The Divorced Land of Sam's
Sam Has Two of Everything Now

Dr. Camille Adams Jones
Illustrated by Calvin Rose II

To order additional copies of this book, contact:
Xlibris
844-714-8691
www.Xlibris.com
Orders@Xlibris.com

ISBN: Softcover   978-1-6641-8805-1
            Hardcover   978-1-6641-8804-4
            EBook   978-1-6641-8806-8

Library of Congress Control Number: 2021915767

Print information available on the last page

Rev. date: 08/26/2021

Dedication

I dedicate this piece with love, regard, and honor to my village. I celebrate every lesson extended at 827 Pepperidge Road; for that light and legacy I am forever grateful. To my Kennedy, Ethan, and Channing: thank you for your love, which arrives each day without conditions or reason. And lastly, to my dream keeper, Jerome. "Unconditional" is an understatement, and there is simply no other hand I ever want to hold in this journey called life.

In a town found beyond many mountains,
hills, lands, and roads, Past several farms,
lakes, ranches, terrains, and zip codes.

There is a village of little girls and
boys who share a special bond.
They come in all shapes and sizes: red
hair, brown hair, and curly blond.

They have blue, hazel, brown and green
eyes and stand short, medium, and tall;
They have small feet and large feet. Some
wear glasses and some don't at all.
These boys and girls are different, but
something about them is the same:

They are all named Sam! Wow, they
all have the same first name.
The Sams also have one more thing in
common in this land where they all live and
roam: They had two of everything because
their parents live in separate homes.

The Sams have two winter hats, two
sets of gloves, and two red sleds;

Two mugs for hot cocoa and two carrots
to put on their two snowmen's heads.

Two swimsuits, two tubes of
sunscreen, and two beach balls;

Two bikes to ride, two skateboards,
and two kites to fly high and tall.

Two blankets, two pillowcases, and
two bedrooms to decorate;

Two places to play hide-and-seek and two
art spaces for the Sams to create.

In their two homes, the Sams finish two plates
of mac and cheese, their favorite meal to eat;

Two movie nights to enjoy, two tubs of popcorn
to share, and two ice-cream sundae treats.

They had two pumpkins to carve
and two costumes to wear as they
get ready for Halloween fun.

Two turkeys and two pans of mashed potatoes
to eat before Thanksgiving Day is done.

Two stockings to hang as the Sams prepare for
the arrival of Santa Claus and his reindeer.

Two birthday wishes to make and two
celebrations of New Year cheer.

Two houses to do their chores in as they work
to keep both Mommy's and Daddy's homes neat;

Two sets of rules to follow, as both parents have expectations for the Sams to meet.

Now, the Sams do have some sadness as they travel to and from their two different homes, Because it is not always fun to have two different toothbrushes and two different combs.

It is not always a happy feeling to have two
different birthday parties and separate holidays;
It did not always please the Sams to have to split
their time since their parents parted ways.

In the beginning it was hard for the Sams
that their parents no longer lived together,

But the best and biggest thing the Sams have is two people who can now love them even better.

Even though their parents live in different places,

The Sams know they are loved in
each of their separate spaces.

The now healthy parents are able to give the
Sams two homes filled with love from the heart;
They are able to show the Sams peace and
harmony in improved ways now that they are apart.

Mommy's and Daddy's homes changed, but their hugs and kisses to their Sams all stayed the same, Even though the parents no longer hug each other and no longer share the same last name.

The mommies and daddies still adore their dearest
Sams very much and work to give them joy.
The Sams are given mounds of love and care
that different homes can never destroy.

Because love travels everywhere regardless of
where the Sams or their parents live or reside,
The happiness, support, and care that mommies
and daddies have can never be erased or set aside.

49 likes

View all 9 comments

So even if the Sams have two of
everything, including a mommy's house and
a daddy's house for the Sams to stay,
No longer living together does not lessen the
parents' love for their Sams in any way.

48 likes

View all 11 comments

Instead, it increases parents chance to build
bonds, shared throughout the Sams' childhoods
As the Sams embrace their two homes and receive
the love their parents give for their greater good.

So smile, Sams! Things are going to be just
fine. There are better days ahead, and
good times will return once again.

There is family fun and new memories to be made in your new two homes, so get ready to settle in.